In **Elmo's World**, one thing always leads to another.

*Library of Congress Cataloging-in-Publication Data*
Alexander, Liza. Flutter By, Butterfly / by Liza Alexander ; illustrated by David Prebenna.
p.   cm. — (Elmo's world ; #2)
Summary: When a butterfly unexpectedly flutters by and surprises Elmo,
it sets off a chain reaction of funny accidents.
ISBN 0-679-88700-8 (trade) — ISBN 0-679-98700-2 (lib. bdg.)
[1. Butterflies—Fiction.  2. Puppets—Fiction.]
I. Prebenna, David, ill.  II. Title.  III. Series.
PZ7.A37735Bu  1998
[E]—dc21  98-12693

www.randomhouse.com/kids
www.sesamestreet.com
CTW BOOKS is a trademark of CTW Publishing Company LLC.

Printed in Mexico.  10 9 8 7 6 5 4 3 2 1

# Flutter By, Butterfly

by Liza Alexander

illustrated by
David Prebenna

**Featuring Jim Henson's Sesame Street Muppets**

CTW Books

Today is a day for silly surprises.
Elmo is playing ball when a butterfly flutters by.
"Ooh, hello, pretty butterfly," says Elmo.

"Oopsie-daisy!" There goes Elmo's ball.

Bouncy,
bouncy,
BOUNCE . . .

Zoe's tall tower of blocks crashes down!

"Wow," says Elmo. "Lucky Elmo's dump truck was handy!"
Elmo and Zoe watch as the blocks tumble into the truck.

"Uh-oh," says Elmo.
The truck is rolling.
The truck is tilting.
The blocks are spilling.
*Clunkety-clunk-clunk!*

"Look out!" Elmo cries.

The truck goes BUMP and knocks open the hamster's cage. "There goes Fluffy!"

"Follow that hamster!" Everyone joins in the chase, but
Fluffy is fast and gets away. Rumbly-bumble, Elmo tumbles.

*Thunk!* Elmo tumbles into the bookshelf. Floppety-flop, the books begin to fall.

"The flowers!" calls Zoe. The vase jiggles off the shelf, and the flowers fly. Elmo catches the vase. Zoe catches the flowers.

Elmo is getting a little tired. Maybe he will take a short rest. He lies down on the rug. Then he sees something strange. There's a bump in the rug—and it's moving!

"It's Fluffy!" says Elmo. The hamster runs out from under the rug into the playhouse. Elmo follows as fast as he can. So do the other little monsters.

"Gotcha!" says Elmo.

Fluffy is saved.

Elmo carries Fluffy back to his cage. Everyone claps and Elmo takes a bow—right into the music stand. It crashes to the floor and the instruments scatter, clatter, *ring-a-ling, ka-bong!*

Everyone makes music. *Root-a-toot-toot! Ting-ting! Clack-clack! Ring-a-ding-ding! Jingle-jangle! Rat-a-tat-tat!*

Flutter by, butterfly...
"Bye-bye!" says Elmo.

In Elmo's world, one thing always leads to another.
Today is a day for silly surprises.